THE ANIMALS OF FARTHING WOOD
Rat Attack!

Colin Dann

University of Hertfordshire

College Lane, Hatfield, Herts. AL10 9AB

Learning and Information Services
de Havilland Campus Learning Resources Centre, Hatfield

For renewal of Standard and One Week Loans,
please visit the web site **http://www.voyager.herts.ac.uk**

Adapted by Sue Mongre
Illustrated by Gary Re
Licensed by BBC Enterpri

RED FOX

White Deer Park had always been a home for every animal that wanted to live there, but no-one expected an army of rats to march in one day...

'Here we are!' called Bully, leader of the rats. 'Welcome to our lovely new home, lads!'

The rats crowded behind their leader and peered over his shoulder, trying to see the Park where they would be living. Bully laughed a horrible laugh to himself and rubbed his paws together. 'You'd better watch out, White Deer Park,' he said. 'Because I've arrived, and I plan to ruuuule!'

The rats were soon disliked by all the other animals living in the Park.

The very first day they arrived, Bully and two of the other rats, Spike and Brat, met Mossy Mole who'd just popped out of one of his molehills.

'What have we here?' snarled Bully nastily. 'It's a little mole, lads! What do you reckon? Bit of a snack now, or shall we save him for lunch?'

Spike and Brat chuckled. 'Don't know about you, boss,' said Brat, 'but I'm feeling rather peckish now!'

Spike licked his lips. 'A mouthful of mole would go down very nicely,' he replied.

It was lucky that Measly was passing at that moment.

It was even luckier that Weasel had just told him how strong and brave he was.

'I'm strong! I'm brave!' he was telling himself over and over again when he saw Mossy surrounded by the vicious-looking rats.

He was feeling so strong and brave that he just charged out of the bushes to save his friend.

Bully, Spike and Brat dropped Mossy immediately.
  'It's a - ' said Spike.
  'It's a - ' said Brat.
  'Run, lads!' said Bully. 'It's a WEASEL!'
  If there was one animal the rats were scared of, it was a weasel.
Without another word, they were off, running for their lives.
Measly was a hero!

Bully and his rats went back to their den in low spirits. If there were going to be weasels around, White Deer Park could be a very dangerous place to live in! Weasels had sharp teeth, could run fast, and didn't like rats!

But later that day, the rats heard weaselly voices and popped up from the bushes to listen. It was Weasel and Measly - and they were leaving the Park!

'Come on, Measly,' Weasel was shouting impatiently. 'Let's get out of here! We can find a better home to live in!'

The rats looked at each other, grinning.

'You know what this means, don't you?' said Bully, flicking his tail happily. 'The Park will be ours!'

Bully sent for more of his rats to move into White Deer Park, and the other animals started to feel very worried. Bully's army was gradually taking over all the space by the pond, and the animals were becoming too frightened to drink there any more.

Fox called a meeting of the animals and they gathered that night around his den.

'The rats are killing all my froggy mateys in the pond!' reported Toad. 'As soon as one of them hops out of the water - munch! - one of those horrible rats has got 'em!'

'They tried to attack me the other day when I was drinking from the pond,' complained Dash the hare. 'Luckily I heard them coming and could get away, but if I hadn't ...' She shivered. No-one liked to think of what might have happened.

'If only the weasels hadn't left!' groaned Fox. 'They'd have helped to sort them out!' He sighed. What were they going to do against this enemy?

Whisper, Charmer and Ranger had a plan. The next night, they crept down to the pond. As they appeared all the rats started panicking and rushing around. Fox alert! Fox alert!

Bully was at the pond on his own, drinking from the water. The three foxes surrounded Bully, growling and showing their teeth. Whisper spoke first. 'We're not going to kill you - this time,' she said. 'Three against one isn't a fair fight, where we come from. We've just come to tell you that you're not welcome in the Park any more. We want you and your rats OUT!'

But instead of taking the warning, Bully just laughed. 'You foxy lot don't frighten me!' he said. 'And it's too late now, anyway, - we're here to stay! This is our patch! The Rat Kingdom!'

Ranger snarled and was about to strike, but Bully was too quick for him and disappeared down one of his rat holes before their eyes.

'We should have killed him while we had the chance,' Ranger growled angrily.

Getting rid of Bully was not going to be easy!

After that, Bully was more and more cocky. 'That White Deer Park lot are nothing but a bunch of softies!' he told the other rats scornfully. 'Those stupid foxes almost had me trapped last night - and they just gave me a warning! Didn't even try to bite me with their sharp foxy teeth! It's going to be a pushover, lads! They're all too nice to try anything!'

The rat takeover spread through the Park. At first, the rats had mostly killed smaller animals that lived near the pond, such as frogs, mice and squirrels. But now they took to coming right into the centre of White Deer Park and hunting in packs, so that none of the animals were safe. Bully even took a group of rats into Fox's den to tell him that the rats would never leave! Something had to be done... but what?

As Bully and the other rats left his den, Fox's heart sank. He was an old fox now. He didn't have all the strength and fighting energy he had in his youth. He sighed heavily, but then stood up. He might be getting old, but he certainly wasn't going to give in to a gang of rats!

He called a meeting for all the animals of White Deer Park and told them they must take action!

That night, the animals gathered by the rats' headquarters. Fox instructed them to try and kill at least six rats each. 'If we keep coming back every night killing six rats each, we'll wipe them out in no time!' he said.

The fight was on!

It was a brave fight. The fox family, the badgers, Adder and Sinuous all killed many rats between them. But there were still so many left!

'We'll never get rid of them!' groaned Ranger the next morning.

Adder and Sinuous decided that they would sort things out. If they were going to beat the rats, they had to get rid of Bully first. Without him, the rat gang would fall apart.

They slid into Bully's nest and slithered up to him.

'Sssurprise!' hissed Adder, flicking out her tongue.

Bully bolted down the nearest tunnel. 'You'll never get me!' he shouted. 'Sort them out, lads!'

There were suddenly hundreds of rats in the nest, squeaking and scrabbling at the snakes. Adder and Sinuous were soon being driven out. Bully, now outside watching the whole thing, chuckled.

'They'll never get me!' he said again.

After the snakes' narrow escape, Fox decided that the animals needed to find some new help, somehow. He came up with a new plan.

'We'll go on attacking the rats every night,' he said. 'But from now on, we'll take all the ones we kill and leave them in front of the warden's cottage. When he sees them there every morning, he'll know that there's a rat problem - and he'll have to do something about it!'

They started that night. When the warden woke up the next morning and saw the pile of dead rats outside his front door, he was shocked! Where had all those rats come from?

Plucky the fox, who was watching, realized that the warden couldn't do anything about the rats if he didn't know where they were living! But then he had an idea. Maybe if he laid a trail of the dead rats leading all the way up to the rat headquarters, the warden would realize what was really happening!

But Bully also had plans. 'I'll not have those horrible slimy snakes slithering up behind me in my own nest,' he said angrily. 'Who do they think they're dealing with?'

He thought for a moment. 'That's what we'll do!' he said at last. 'We'll have a snake-hunt! A great, huge snake-hunt! Laaads!'

But the great snake-hunt was going to have to wait because the warden suddenly appeared with a huge shotgun! He had followed the trail of dead rats that the foxes had laid that morning all the way to the rat nests, and now he meant to finish them off.

'Bang!' went the gun. 'Bang! Bang!'

'Quick! Ratties!' screamed Bully. 'Ruuuun!'

Fox and the others were pleased that their plan seemed to have worked. But what they didn't know was that the warden hadn't actually managed to shoot any of the rats - and worse still, Bully was more determined than ever to win.

One of Bully's spies reported that Sinuous was fast asleep in the Park, and Bully decided to get his revenge on the snakes. With the army of rats suddenly upon him, Sinuous really didn't stand a chance. He was dead within seconds.

When Adder found her mate that afternoon lying lifeless and still, she was heartbroken.

The warden came back the next day and put rat poison in the nest.
But one greedy fat rat ate all the poisoned pellets, so that idea
didn't work at all. Fox was getting more and more disheartened.
Would they ever be able to get rid of the rats?

  Bully heard about the poisoning later that day. 'If they're going
to fight dirty, then so will we!' he said. He and the troops went
out there and then, and attacked Toad. 'We'll show you White
Deer Park lot!' shouted Bully.

It was lucky that Mossy Mole was nearby so he could raise the alarm and get some of the other animals to help Toad. White Deer Park was becoming more and more dangerous every day!

Bully knew this, too. He knew that the other animals were getting tired and losing confidence. 'Not long now, my lads!' he kept saying to the other rats. 'Not long now until White Deer Park becomes the Rat Kingdom!'

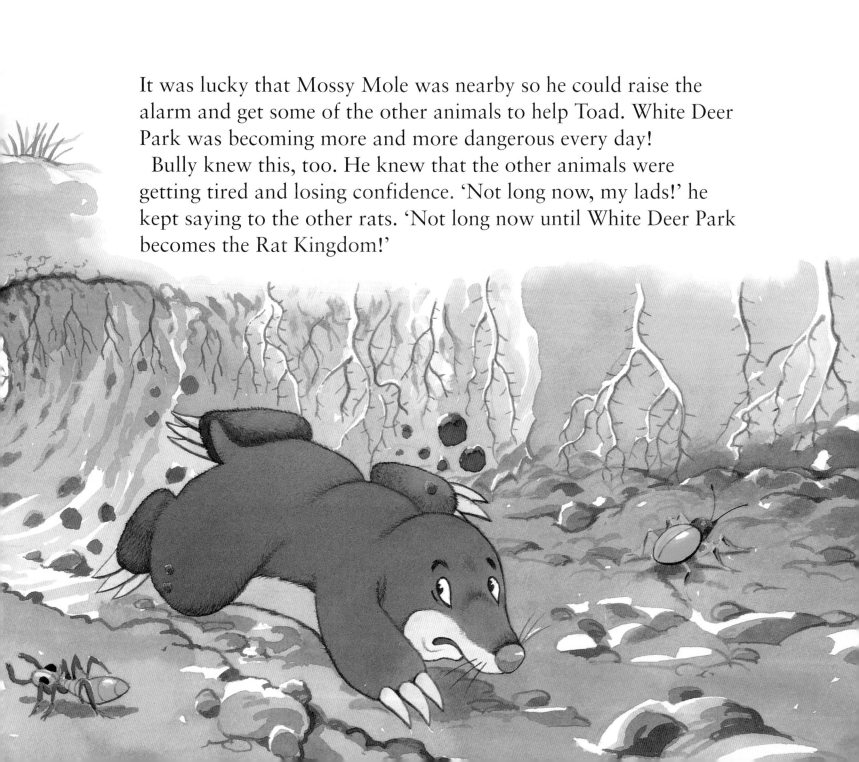

But Bully didn't know about some animals who were returning to the Park. First to arrive were Weasel and her family. They had had all sorts of adventures in the outside world but now they were back, and here to stay.

'My family are excellent rat-catchers!' said Weasel proudly. 'Don't worry - I'll get them on the case immediately!'

Next to return were Owl and her mate Hollow. They flew over the park just as Bully was instructing his troops. They stopped and listened in horror as they heard his plans to take over the Park. What was going on?

'What has happened to the Park while I've been away?' sniffed Owl. 'They just can't manage without me! I'll have to organize the animals right away! It's lucky I'm back!'

Fox and the others were delighted to see Owl and the weasels back. Together they decided how they would battle against the rats.

The weasels distracted the rats from one side. Owl, Hollow and Whistler divebombed them from the air. Just when the rats were getting confused, the foxes and badgers attacked them from behind and drove them all into the pond!

'It's up to you, Bully,' said Fox as the rats began to drown. 'You can gather what's left of your troops and go, or we'll keep fighting until you're all dead. Which is it to be?'

Bully knew he was beaten. He and his rats left the Park there and then.

The other animals breathed a tired sigh of relief as they watched the rats leaving. They had won the battle! And White Deer Park was a safe place to live once more.

A RED FOX BOOK
Published by Random House Children's Books
20 Vauxhall Bridge Road, London SW1V 2SA

A division of Random House UK Ltd
London Melbourne Sydney Auckland Johannesburg
and agencies throughout the world

First published by Red Fox 1995
Text and illustrations © Random House UK Ltd 1995

Based on the animation series produced by
Telemagination/La Fabrique for the
BBC/European Broadcasting Union
from the series of books about
The Animals of Farthing Wood by Colin Dann

Set in Sabon 16pt/20pt

Printed in Slovenia
by Mladinska Knjiga

Random House UK Limited Reg. No. 954009.

Animals of Farthing Wood Logotype © European
Broadcasting Union 1992. Licensed by BBC Enterprises Ltd

The Animals of Farthing Wood logotype is a trade mark
of BBC Enterprises Ltd and is used under licence.

ISBN 0 09 952281 0